CUPID
and
PSYCHE

AS TOLD BY
M. CHARLOTTE CRAFT

ILLUSTRATED BY
K. Y. CRAFT

MORROW JUNIOR BOOKS ❋ NEW YORK

Oil over watercolor
was used for the full-color illustrations.
The text type is 18-point Opti Eve.

Printed in the United States of America.
1 2 3 4 5 6 7 8 9 10

Library of Congress Cataloging-in-Publication Data
Craft, Marie Charlotte.
Cupid and Psyche / retold by Marie Charlotte Craft;
illustrated by Kinuko Y. Craft.
p. cm.
Summary: The god of love, Cupid, falls
in love with a beautiful mortal, Psyche.
ISBN 0-688-13163-8 (trade)
ISBN 0-688-13164-6 (library)
[1. Cupid (Roman deity).   2. Psyche (Greek deity).
3. Mythology, Greek.]   I. Craft, Kinuko, ill.   II. Title.
BL820.C65C73 1996   398.2'1—dc20
95-14895   CIP AC

For Marianna Mayer

There once lived a king and queen who were blessed with three daughters. All three were lovely, but the youngest, Psyche, was the most beautiful of all. So great was her beauty that word spread throughout the neighboring lands that she was actually Venus, the goddess of beauty herself, living among mortals. Soon people were traveling from far and wide to offer her their gifts and prayers.

In spite of this attention, Psyche was unhappy. Her two sisters had long since married, each to a king. But no king, prince, or even lowly pauper dared ask for Psyche's hand. She remained alone, admired by all but loved by none.

So famous was Psyche's beauty that Venus's temple was deserted and her statues stood ignored. The goddess was furious that her beauty should be challenged by that of a mere mortal. She called for her son, Cupid, the handsome and mischievous god of love. His golden arrows were feared even by the gods, for their lightest touch inspired love at first sight. "You must avenge this insult to me," Venus commanded. "Use your arrows to make that worthless girl fall madly in love with the most frightening creature in the world!"

Cupid, always eager for a chance to create mischief, made himself invisible and hastened to Psyche's chamber, where he found her fast asleep. As he was fitting an arrow to his bow, Psyche opened her eyes and seemed to look directly at him. Startled, Cupid nicked himself with his own arrow and instantly fell in love. Unable to keep his promise to Venus, he fled.

That morning, Psyche journeyed to Delphi to ask the oracle of Apollo whether it was her fate to remain alone. "You will wed," the oracle replied, "but to a creature feared by the gods themselves. You must go to the top of the nearest mountain. There you will meet your fate."

Psyche returned home and bid good-bye to her grieving family. "Surely," she said, "this creature cannot be worse than a life of loneliness." Then, accompanied by the mournful sounds of funeral songs and her family's tears, Psyche climbed to the summit. In spite of all her brave words, she stood trembling as she awaited the arrival of her monstrous husband.

Quickly a fog swirled around Psyche, and she felt the warm breath of Zephyrus, the gentle west wind. He lifted her down the mountain and over its treacherous rocks and laid her safely on a bed of flowers in a distant valley.

Before her she saw a palace more beautiful and elegant than any she had ever seen. Stepping cautiously through the doorway, she found rooms filled with every imaginable luxury. No need had been overlooked, no detail forgotten.

A gentle voice whispered, "The house and all it contains are yours. Do as you wish. Dinner awaits you when it pleases you to eat." Psyche turned to see who had spoken, but there was no one in the room.

That evening, refreshed and rested, Psyche entered the grand banquet hall, where a long table was laid with exquisite delicacies. She dined alone, attended by invisible servants and soothed by the sweet songs of unseen musicians.

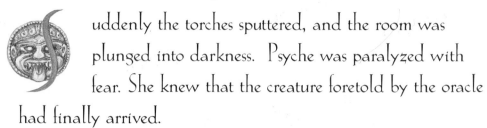uddenly the torches sputtered, and the room was plunged into darkness. Psyche was paralyzed with fear. She knew that the creature foretold by the oracle had finally arrived.

But the voice that greeted her was kind. "Do not be afraid, dearest Psyche," he whispered gently. "I mean you no harm." As they talked, her unseen companion calmed her fears, and soon she began to smile, then to laugh, until finally she quite forgot her terror.

And so Psyche began her new life. She passed her days doing as she pleased, and in the evenings, her unseen companion devised new pastimes and adventures for her enjoyment. He denied her only one thing: the chance to see him. Psyche teased and begged, but nothing she could do or say would persuade him otherwise. "I would rather that you love me for what I am," he said, "not for what I appear to be."

As Psyche grew accustomed to her new life, she thought often of her family, knowing that they wept for her as lost. She asked if her sisters might be brought to visit her. Although reluctant at first, her host was moved by her pleas and consented. But he warned, "You must tell them nothing of me, or all we share here will be lost."

he next morning, Psyche called for Zephyrus to fetch
her sisters. Upon being reunited, all three wept for
joy. But her sisters' joy quickly turned to envy as
Psyche proudly showed off her new home. They thought it
unjust that she, the youngest, should be blessed with both beauty
and wealth. Hoping to find some unhappiness in Psyche's new
life, they questioned her about their absent host.

"Where is he?" demanded one sister.

"Why can we not meet him?" complained the other.

As her sisters persisted, Psyche first told them that their
host was sick and could not rise from his bed to greet them.
Later, when her sisters questioned her further, Psyche said that
he was away on important business. But still her sisters would
not cease their questioning, until finally, on the day they were to
return to their husbands, Psyche confessed that while her host
was generous and kind in all other things, she was forbidden to
see him. "He is the creature the oracle promised!" the sisters
cried. "Tonight, when he is asleep, you must look at him. If he
is a hideous beast, you must kill him, before he can kill you!"

hat night, Psyche did her best to ignore her sisters' advice, but their talk of the oracle had brought back all her fears.

When she was sure her host was asleep, she lit a lamp and slipped into his chamber with a knife. As the lamplight flickered across the face of her sleeping host, Psyche was astonished to find not a monster but Cupid, the beautiful god of love himself. Curious, she reached out to touch one of the arrows that lay in a quiver at his feet and quite accidentally pricked herself. And turning back to look at Cupid, she fell in love.

As she leaned forward to kiss his lips, a drop of hot oil spilled from her lamp, burning Cupid's shoulder. With a cry, he awoke and saw the knife that she still held in her hand. Sadly he told Psyche, "Go back to your sisters. Love cannot live without trust." And with those words he vanished.

iserable, Psyche returned to her sisters, who consoled her while secretly rejoicing at her ill fortune. Day after day, Psyche made offerings and prayed to the gods to be reunited with Cupid. When her prayers went unanswered, Psyche decided she must go to the temple of Venus, in the hope that she might find Cupid there.

No sooner had Psyche left than her foolish sisters rushed to the top of the mountain, each demanding that Zephyrus carry her to the palace as Cupid's new bride. With confidence, they stepped into the swirling fog, expecting the west wind to bear them up. But Zephyrus was not awaiting them, and they fell to their deaths on the rocks below.

upid had fled to his mother in pain, wounded by both the burning oil and Psyche's betrayal. As she tended her son, Venus was more determined than ever to seek revenge on the beautiful mortal.

When Psyche arrived, Venus said, "First you presume to challenge my beauty. Then you wound my son, and yet you would take him from me again. To gain my forgiveness and Cupid's love, you must complete three tasks. If you fail, you will never see him again." With that, Venus led the girl to a huge room filled with grain. "Sort these mountains of grain into three separate piles of barley, wheat, and millet by sunset."

As the door was shut behind her, Psyche desperately tried to pick through the mounds, but she made no progress. Then, spying a band of ants passing through on their way to the fields, she cried, "My friends, if you would help me sort this grain, I would gladly share it with you." Soon the ants were scurrying about, separating the grains and sorting each to its own pile, and taking only a handful as their reward. At dusk, Venus was far from pleased to find the task completed.

The next morning Venus said, "Here is a simple chore. In the grove beyond the river you will find a herd of sheep with fleece of gold. Bring me an armful of their fleece!"

Relieved to be given so easy a task, Psyche immediately set off. As she was debating how best to cross the river, she came across a young sparrow who had fallen from its nest. Taking it gently in her hand, Psyche returned it to the nest. In gratitude the sparrow's mother warned, "If you try to gather the golden fleece now, the fierce rams will destroy you with their sharp horns and hooves. Better to wait until midday, when they leave the riverbanks for the shade of the woods. Then you may gather all the fleece you desire from what they have left behind on the bushes."

When Psyche returned safely with her arms full of golden fleece, Venus was furious. Masking her anger with a smile, she said casually, "For your third task, take this box to Queen Proserpine in the land of the dead. Tell her I am weary from tending my son and that I need a little beauty for myself."

ow recovered from his wounds, Cupid was touched by Psyche's determination to win him back. Although greatly afraid of what might befall her in the underworld, Cupid was prevented by his mother's powers from joining Psyche on her journey. He made himself invisible and flew to Psyche's side, with careful instructions about reaching Proserpine's palace and returning again. He handed Psyche two gold coins and six honey cakes and warned her that she should stop for nothing, speak to no one other than Proserpine, and eat nothing, no matter how hungry she became. No one must know that she was from the land of the living. "My love," he said, "do not allow your curiosity to get the better of you. Should you forget anything I have told you, you will never return."

Her heart pounding, Psyche stepped through the mouth of the cave that concealed the path to the underworld. She slowly made her way down the steep path, stopping only when she reached the dark waters of the river Styx. There she allowed the ghostly ferryman, Charon, to pluck a gold coin from her lips as payment for her journey to the opposite bank. She knew that if she used her hands to pay Charon, he would know she was alive and would not allow her to cross the river. Once she reached the opposite shore, an old man on a lame donkey called out to her for help. But mindful of Cupid's warning, Psyche hurried on. At the gates to the palace, she fed the fearsome three-headed dog, Cerberus, three honey cakes and was allowed to enter.

Once inside the palace, Psyche found that Proserpine had set a banquet in her honor, but she ate nothing, taking only the box that the queen returned to her.

areful to thank Proserpine for her kindness, Psyche began her journey back. She fed Cerberus the remaining honey cakes and was allowed through the palace gates. Remembering to pay Charon his gold coin from her lips, Psyche was ferried back across the Styx. After scrabbling up the rocky path, it was with great joy that she stepped into the bright daylight of the living.

Looking at the box, Psyche wondered if perhaps she might take just a little beauty in order to make herself as lovely as possible for Cupid. Eagerly, she opened the box but found it empty of beauty; it contained only the sleep of the dead. Psyche's eyes closed, and she fell to the ground.

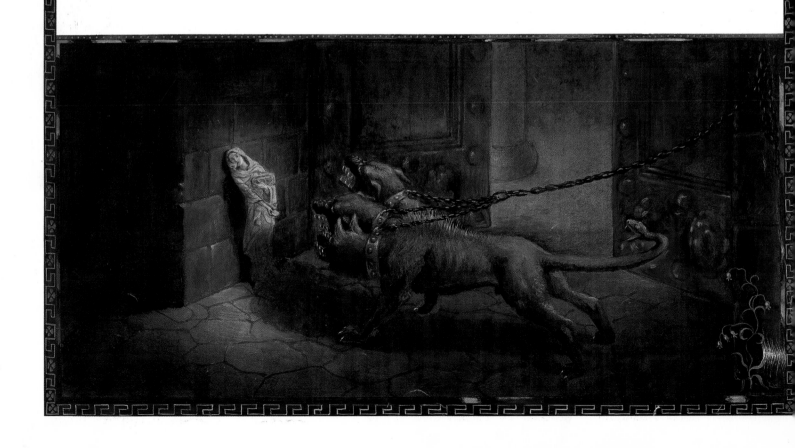

hen he saw his beloved fall, Cupid flew to her side. He drew the sleep from her eyes and placed it back in the box, closing it tightly.

Now that the three tasks were completed, Cupid was no longer under his mother's power. He became visible again and woke Psyche with a kiss.

"Oh, Cupid," she cried, "having lost you once, I wish never to lose you again. Can you forgive me?"

"Only if you will forgive me, dearest Psyche," he answered. "I should not have left you, and I never will again. You are my soul."

ith a light heart, Psyche went to deliver Proserpine's box to Venus. Meanwhile, Cupid flew straight to Olympus. Jupiter, father of all the gods, had found himself in many foolish situations through Cupid's mischief, so he was greatly pleased to see the young god of love caught by his own arrows. Jupiter summoned Psyche and before the entire heavenly assembly presented her with a cup of ambrosia. "Drink this," he told her, "and become immortal. May Cupid and Psyche forever be bound together."

hus, Cupid and Psyche were finally wed, and in due time they had a daughter, whom they called Joy.